**Put Beginning Readers on the Right Track with ALL ABOARD READING™**

The All Aboard Reading series is especially for beginning readers. Written by noted authors and illustrated in full color, these are books that children really and truly *want* to read—books to excite their imagination, tickle their funny bone, expand their interests, and support their feelings. With three different reading levels, All Aboard Reading lets you choose which books are most appropriate for your children and their growing abilities.

**Level 1—for Preschool through First Grade Children**
Level 1 books have very few lines per page, very large type, easy words, lots of repetition, and pictures with visual "cues" to help children figure out the words on the page.

**Level 2—for First Grade to Third Grade Children**
Level 2 books are printed in slightly smaller type than Level 1 books. The stories are more complex, but there is still lots of repetition in the text and many pictures. The sentences are quite simple and are broken up into short lines to make reading easier.

**Level 3—for Second Grade through Third Grade Children**
Level 3 books have considerably longer texts, use harder words and more complicated sentences.

All Aboard for happy reading!

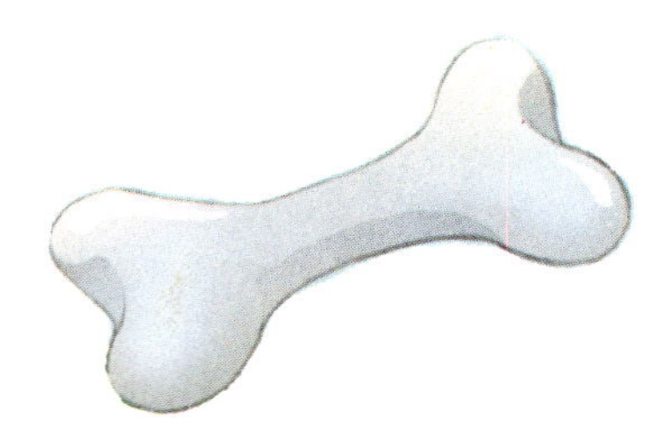

For my parents, with love—G.H.

For Becky and Lizzie—N.G.

 Published by Grosset & Dunlap, Inc., which is a member of The Putnam & Grosset Group, New York. ALL ABOARD READING is a trademark of The Putnam & Grosset Group. GROSSET & DUNLAP is a trademark of Grosset & Dunlap, Inc. Published simultaneously in Canada. Printed in the U.S.A.

*Library of Congress Cataloging-in-Publication Data*
Herman, Gail, 1959- What a hungry puppy! / by Gail Herman ; illustrated by Norman Gorbaty.
p. cm. — (All aboard reading) Summary: Lucky the puppy searches for a bone with surprising results. [1. Dogs—Fiction.] I. Gorbaty, Norman, ill. II. Title. III. Series.
PZ7.H4315Wg 1993 [E]—dc20 92-24468 CIP AC

ISBN 0-448-40537-7 (GB) A B C D E F G H I J
ISBN 0-448-40536-9 (pbk.) B C D E F G H I J

Level 1
Preschool–Grade 1

# WHAT A HUNGRY PUPPY!

By Gail Herman
Illustrated by Norman Gorbaty

Grosset & Dunlap • New York

Lucky is going out
to play.
"Do not go far,"
his boy says.
"It is almost
time for dinner."

Dinner!

All at once,

Lucky is hungry.

Sniff, sniff.

Dig, dig.

Maybe he can find a bone.

But there is no bone.
Just a jump rope.

Lucky walks down the street.
Sniff, sniff, sniff.
Is there a bone
by this tree?

Dig, dig, dig.
Lucky pulls something up.
Is it a bone?
No.
It is an old shoe.
A shoe does not
taste very good.
So Lucky goes on.

Walk, walk, walk.

Sniff, sniff, sniff.

Lucky smells something—

right here!

Lucky digs and digs.
Up comes something...

but it is only a sock.

A smelly old sock.

Lucky walks a little more.

Sniff, sniff, sniff.

Dig, dig, dig.

At last!

Lucky has found it.

Lucky has found a bone!

Lucky looks up.

Oh, no!

He sees a dog.

A big dog.

Lucky is hungry.

But he is scared, too.

Lucky drops the bone.
He runs.
The dog runs, too.
The big dog
runs after Lucky.

Lucky runs past
the smelly sock,
the old shoe,
and the jump rope.
He is home.
But the big dog
is right behind him!

G-r-r-r!
The big dog
is coming closer.
G-r-r-r!
And closer.

Now they are
almost nose to nose!

What does the big dog do?
He licks Lucky.
He is thanking Lucky
for finding his bone.

Lucky wags his tail.
The big dog
is nice.
G-r-r-r!

Then what is that sound?

It is Lucky's tummy.

He is hungry.

Very hungry.

All at once,
Lucky hears his boy.
"Lucky!
Oh, Lucky!"
he calls.
"Dinner is ready."

Lucky starts to run.
Not because he is scared.

Because it is
time for dinner!